Damsel's Dilemma

For Astrid and Robby

Damsel's Dilemma

Elaine Drew

TAERAN

ARTS

Taeran Arts   Pleasanton, California

Taeran Arts, Pleasanton, CA 94566 USA

DAMSEL'S DILEMMA

ISBN 978-0-9833236-4-8

Story and Artwork by Elaine Drew

DEDICATION

To all whose frogs,
in time,
turned into princes

*L*ong ago in a faraway land, a wealthy merchant needed to broach a delicate topic with his daughter. He knocked at her bedroom door. She grunted something or other, he wasn't sure what. He took it as an invitation to enter.

His daughter Eva was sprawled across her bed, staring up at the painted ceiling. The father shifted his weight from foot to foot. He criticized the new cook, who put onions in every dish and couldn't tell a parsnip from a turnip. He went into more detail than required about a tapestry he was commissioning.

"Out with it, Daddy," said Eva. "You didn't come in here to natter on about the household."

"Your mother has told me your monthlies have begun. It's time you married," said Aldrich.

Eva gave him the look she felt the suggestion deserved. Her father left, stymied but undeterred.

Aldrich, who could well afford it, organized an ample dowry the next day and spread the word. He was determined to entice the sort of high-born young man he could welcome into the family. It shouldn't be a problem, he reasoned. After all, the maiden was beautiful and talented. She could spin and embroider, paint and write. Her horsemanship was legendary. She could out ride any man in the realm.

The problem was that even though she could out ride any man, she didn't often choose to. The boys admired her skill. They loved gazing into her emerald eyes and getting lost in her long, glossy chestnut hair. She was one hell of a good time. But she wasn't someone they could bring home to mother.

Months went by, and as they passed, the father's disappointment mounted. When no suitable young man, cap in hand, knocked at the hall door, Aldrich put out some feelers and got wind of his daughter's reputation. He thought it over. He discussed the matter with his wife Hilda.

Aldrich had convinced himself to look on the bright side. "If she starts attending mass, takes some food to the poor, and embroiders a few maniples, people will overlook these little lapses. This will blow over once she starts behaving," he suggested.

"She'll start behaving when you lock her in a tower," said the girl's mother.

The father sought out the maiden. "Look here, Eva. This won't do. If you don't stop planking every boy in cross-gartered hose, I will have to take steps."

Eva put on the guileless look she had perfected. "I'm sorry, Daddy. I didn't mean to distress you."

"Your mother is completely out of patience."

"I know I've been a little naughty, but Mother doesn't understand. The boys are so enthusiastic, and I do hate to disappoint."

"Do you want to go to a convent?"

"Oh, Daddy, you wouldn't. You know how dreary and dried up those women are. They shear off their hair, and their cheeks suck in like they've just eaten an unripe persimmon. They do nothing but sing and pray in chapel, night and day."

"A little praying would do you good," said her father.

"Their skin turns sallow from all that interrupted sleep. They

reek of rancid oil. And they wear the most dreary clothes on earth." Eva was close to tears and gave her father a look that could melt the heart of a charging aurochs. "Surely you wouldn't wish that for me."

"What I wish for you is a solid marriage that will produce fine boys and girls for me to spoil. You must restore your good name." He told Eva the steps she must take.

"Of course, Daddy. I will do every one."

Eva did go to Church the next Sunday, but the ladies of the parish noticed she dozed off more than once. She started an embroidery. It sat in its frame, languishing, with only its stem stitch outline. On Tuesday she delivered food to the village poor. Her mother noticed that it took an unreasonable amount of time for the girl to return.

When Eva finally walked through the door, she tried to sidle to her room unseen. Her mother blocked the girl's path.

"Hi, Mommy."

"Turn around," said Hilda. The back of Eva's gown was stained a vivid grass green.

The mother found Aldrich. "Your daughter has not changed."

"Now, Hilda, let's give it some time. You remember when we were young?"

"That was different," she sniffed. She smiled a little, though.

One night, long after the family was tucked up in bed, there was a loud crash. The father, his steward, and a groomsman ran into the courtyard and spied a young man sprawled over the hedge.

"What are you doing here?" growled the father. The boy was silent.

"Get the sheriff," the father said to his man.

"No, no!" said the boy. "You know who I am." He worked on a

nearby neighbor's estate, a handsome lad with the thigh muscles of a horseman.

"What are you doing skulking about my garden?"

The father glanced up to his daughter's bedroom and noticed the open window. The boy stammered and fidgeted. "Get out of here!" bellowed the father.

Aldrich marched up to Eva's room. "That's it!" he said. "I'm locking you in the tower."

This time her pleading and her promises to reform fell on deaf ears. Once she realized her entreaties were useless, she switched from cajolery to insult. Aldrich and his two men had a difficult time restraining the girl as they trundled her up the tower's 414 steps. The men, too winded for conversation, pushed her into the small room at the top and bolted the door from the outside.

Later that day Aldrich had the tower enclosed with a spiked wall and posted a guard at its only gate. To be on the safe side, he hired an old woman to watch the guard.

For the time being, until his negotiations were finished, Aldrich was sure that seclusion was the best, indeed the only feasible, policy. Each day, the maiden glared out her one small window. Once the father had cooled off, he had the servants take her tasty tidbits, although Hilda maintained that bread and water would be more suitable.

One morning Aldrich ventured into the courtyard. He called up to his daughter, "I wouldn't do this if I didn't love you." Eva threw a half-eaten apple in his direction.

"The guard, not to mention the extra pay to get servants to trudge up so many steps, is costing your mother and me a fortune!" Aldrich dodged a mildewed trencher.

"I don't want to marry!"

"If you had some self-control this wouldn't be necessary."

She refused to talk to him and barred her door from the inside so he couldn't get in. One day when she spied him in the courtyard she threw a clear yellow liquid in his direction. Even so, the man remained a soft touch for the girl. He brooded over her hostility. "I know, Hilda," he said, "let's send her some gifts to cheer her up."

"Send her whatever you like," said her mother. "As for me, I'll send her a switch so she can beat herself."

The father began sending little presents to his daughter, one every other day. First he sent an illuminated prayer book. She looked at the pictures and then hurled it at a young shepherd who was passing beneath her window. When the beautiful book landed on his shoulder, the boy thought it came from heaven, renounced his sins, and vowed to join a monastery.

Aldrich sent her a silver thimble, and Eva pitched it at the back of the daydreaming guard's head. The man blushed bright red, thinking someone had read his thoughts.

One day her father sent Eva a small apple made of pure gold, a carved cherrywood box, and an unusual, beautiful little snake. Aldrich had bought these from a foreign merchant who told him the serpent had magic powers to bring its owner good luck. And perhaps it did, but it took a while.

When Eva unwrapped the golden apple she flung it across the room. She set the wooden box near the window so she could throw it at her father the next time he stepped into the courtyard. But when she saw the snake, she was enchanted. She couldn't resist playing with him and feeding him little scraps of food. She named him Wermhere. The little snake slithered over to the window and curled up inside the wooden box.

Eva thought Wermhere looked so sweet in there that instead of throwing the box at her father, she kept it. Wermhere crawled around her chamber, exploring his new domain like a kitten. When he found the gold apple, he wound himself around it and went to sleep.

Eva noticed how much Wermhere liked the apple, so she put it in his box. Eva found herself talking to the little snake all day, and from his intelligent expression, she was sure he understood. She was glad for the companionship. Eva told him he was the first friend who listened to her.

They whiled away the days, playing games like hide and seek. Looking for Wermhere under her bed one afternoon, she discovered an ancient chess set and tried to teach her new friend to play. That worked out about as well as you might expect. Eva didn't mind.

After a week or so, a strange thing began to happen. The snake was growing, which seemed natural at first. But one day Eva noticed that the golden apple was growing as well. At first, she thought she must be imagining it. She began to observe closely. She traced the apple's outline on the wall. She waited a week and then compared the apple to her sketch. There was no doubt about it, Eva realized, the apple was larger.

In two more weeks, the snake and the apple had both outgrown the cherry wood box, and within two months, the apple took up most of Eva's room. When the snake coiled around it, his head bumped against the ceiling.

Eva pondered what to do. She didn't want to let her companion leave, but when his head began to crack the ceiling, she realized she must.

The snake loved the maiden as much as she loved him, so while he didn't resist going outside, he refused to leave the compound.

He took up his post, his body encircling the tower. Once outside, the snake began to change. Finlike wings sprouted from his back, and he grew legs with long, clawed paws. When he was hungry, as he often was, he roared, and fire came out of his mouth. He was no longer a snake. He had become a dragon.

Meanwhile, Aldrich had been busy. During the time his daughter was safely secluded, he had found a lord who hadn't heard of Eva's loose ways. He and his wife had been traveling the world while Eva had been busy ruining her reputation. The trip abroad had cost the lord a lot. The idea of a handsome dowry appealed. Aldrich arranged a match with the lord's son, and, being a merchant, he bargained well. Granted, the boy was a second son, but his older brother was sickly.

All had seemed settled, but with a dragon surrounding the tower, Aldrich couldn't deliver the maiden. No one dared enter the enclosure. The fence was scorched by the dragon's frequent complaints about tardy mealtimes. The lord who had promised his son broke off the match. He said his son couldn't wait forever, you know. Aldrich was beside himself. He tried to interest the local youth in helping him free his daughter, but they all said that while she was lovely and great company, they really had to be leaving to campaign against those blood-thirsty Peckies or to squash the marauding Wigesta or something equally pressing.

One day the golden apple, which had been growing larger each day just like the dragon, became so heavy that it rolled along the floor of Eva's room and broke through the wall. So now, in addition to the dragon, the maiden's courtyard contained an enormous apple of pure gold. This was the first the father knew of the apple.

When he saw it, he realized it offered the best hope of a solution to his problem. Aldrich let it be known that any man who could kill the dragon that imprisoned his daughter would be privileged to have both her hand and the golden apple.

A year went by, and no one responded to his generous offer. Eva was getting chilly with a hole in the wall. The girl would talk to her father now when he came to the edge of the fence and hollered up to her. "My life is ruined," she wailed, "and it's all your fault."

Things were about to take a turn. In a distant kingdom, there lived an old king. He had spent his entire fortune fighting his rotten and covetous neighbors. Unfortunately, funding an army is not cheap. He had taxed his people as much as he dared. Not only would his conscience prick him if he asked for more, there was a good chance he'd have a rebellion at home as well as a war on his border. Things were looking grim. If the king didn't find some source of revenue to fund the lavish gifts necessary to buy fighting men, his kingdom would soon become a fiefdom of this hateful tribe.

This king had a son who was known for valor. The youth was as merciless to the enemy as he was generous to his friends. And he was good-looking, too. The king called this son to him and explained the situation.

"Father," said Prince Eric, "do not expect to see me again until I come to you with enough gold to pay all our warriors and buy all those of our enemies." With those brave words, he gathered a troop of twelve loyal companions.

The lads spent a number of days hanging about the mead hall, bragging about the undertaking. They prevailed upon the tender

feelings of their soon-to-be-abandoned girlfriends, and more than one surrendered her virginity. When the boys could put it off no longer, they dressed in their spanking new armor, mounted their steeds, and headed for the border.

The band traveled for several months, raiding the peasant hamlets of nearby kingdoms and stealing just about enough food to stay alive. The boys threatened the locals with all sorts of unpleasant procedures as they tried to extract information, but no one seemed to know where they could find a rich but poorly defended castle to conquer.

Then one day, far from home, Prince Eric came to a village, intent on pillage. An old woman approached his horse. The story of the golden apple had spread as far as this, and the crone had heard it. She was clever as well as crafty, so while the men of her village ran around arming themselves with scythes and pickaxes, she sallied forth to divert their attackers.

"Spare us," she said, "and I will tell you how to get more gold than you can ever use."

The prince, not an unreasonable lad, lowered his sword and listened. The old woman told him about the maiden in the tower and the golden apple. She didn't mention the dragon. The woman said that the father had promised both the apple and the daughter to the first man who could convince his daughter to marry him. Being analytical, the old woman had figured out that either the prince would be killed by the dragon, which was fine with her, or he would kill the dragon, get the gold, and go back where he came from, which was also fine with her.

The old woman soon discovered that this young fellow was not as dim as he looked. The prince said, "That's all well and good, Madam Crone, but we all know that maidens in towers and golden apples are invariably guarded by dragons. Why else would that apple of pure gold be there for the taking? I'm sorry, but fighting those beasts is not in my portfolio. They have very sharp claws, and don't they breathe fire?"

"My boy, I mean Your Royal Highness, I haven't heard a peep about any dragon."

"Let's say," said the prince, "that something was left out of the story by the time it made its way to your village."

"Bosh and poppycock. No one would leave out anything that interesting. But if there should happen to be a dragon, I can tell you that folks in these parts have been fighting those beasts for centuries. They are nothing to fret over or worry about. Defeating a dragon is as easy as picking plums in summer."

"Tell me more, Madam Crone."

"We have some tricks up our sleeves. They have never failed. And you have to admit that a huge apple of pure gold, not to mention a beautiful maiden, is worth some risk."

The prince had to admit that the apple probably was worth taking a chance for. As for the girl, he wasn't so sure. He had no interest in the bother of a wife, and if he changed his mind, there were plenty of girls back home. As far as he could tell, they all wanted to marry the next king. In the meantime, they were as accommodating as could be.

The old woman said, "I'm glad to see that little smile on your face, my boy."

The lad realized his mind had wandered. He pulled himself back to the problem at hand. "Tell me your tricks," he said.

"As a skilled warrior you know how to use a sword and a spear. The best technique is to thrust your spear, well aimed, right into his heart."

"How can I get close enough to do that without being burned alive by his fiery breath?"

"If you and your friends mind your manners, I will sew you just the thing you need."

The prince conferred with his friends, and they decided that this was a venture worth pursuing. They stayed with the old woman for three days. They weren't allowed to wear their boots in her house or put their elbows on the table, either. When it was time for them to leave, the old woman gave the prince a long tunic made of two layers of leather, dipped in pitch and stuffed with heavy fleece. The crone wasn't sure whether the pitch on the outside would protect him or make the fire hotter, and she didn't care.

She gave Prince Eric the most confusing directions she could think of. She sent him far out of the way on a circuitous route. It would have been a disaster if the ruffians found out that she was lying about the dragon. Plus, if things didn't work out, she didn't want him to find his way back.

The prince and his band proceeded on their way with the typical sort of mishaps and grumbling and dissension that you might imagine. There was a day when rain and blinding hail made it impossible to travel. A flooded river was too high to cross, and it took the boys two days to build a bridge. They got lost in a forest. When they killed a stag for dinner, a warden caught them, and it took the last of their money to bribe him enough to avoid his lord's justice. But finally, tired and bedraggled, they got closer to the right kingdom, and as they did, it became apparent that something strange was going on. The maiden, the tower, and the dragon were the talk of all the neighboring villages.

They asked their way again and again. Everyone knew the way to the maiden's tower. Unfortunately, not everyone knew the same way, so the noble warriors got lost a few more times before they found themselves staring at a scorched wooden wall against whose inside edges pressed a large and vicious dragon. How he roared when he heard them!

The prince gathered his troop. "Let's leave this until nightfall. Reptiles are cold-blooded. It won't be able to move as fast."

After dark, he donned the protective gear the old woman had made for him. His friends said they would stand ready, for sure, right outside the wall.

"Stand ready for what?" said the prince. "Does not one of you have the courage to come in with me?"

"If you get in trouble we'll be right here," said one. "It makes no sense for all of us to get burned, and you're the only one with a flame-proof vest." The others nodded their heads in agreement.

He left his companions near the scorched wall and sneaked inside. As soon as he went through the gate he tripped over the dragon, who awakened and roared a fierce roar with its hot breath. The prince could feel the heat on his face, but, almost miraculously, his body was protected by his bulky leather garment. The dragon tried to lash at the lad with its tail and slash him with its sharp claws and bite him with its razor-like teeth, but Wermhere could do none of these things. For one thing, he was draped awkwardly over the giant apple. Each time he stirred, the apple rolled, and he couldn't get any leverage. Besides that, his body was so tightly wedged between the tower and the fence that he could hardly budge.

Eva was awakened by the commotion and looked out the window. What a jumble of emotions she felt. She wanted to be released from her prison, but she didn't want to see her dear friend, the dragon, killed. She wanted a man, but she wanted to have some choice in the matter. On lonely nights she sometimes pushed down a secret longing that a handsome prince would come along and rescue her, fall in love with her, beg her to come

away with him to his kingdom. When she was feeling more rational, she realized that she wanted to spend that huge lump of gold herself. Now it might go to this ridiculous knight, who looked thoroughly dumpy in his baggy leather fleece.

"Get the hell out of here, you interfering bastard," she screamed at the prince.

The prince lifted his spear and drove it into Wermhere's long spine. The dragon wrenched his body around. His back was on the ground, his stumpy legs in the air, his soft belly exposed. The lad drove his spear into the dragon's loins and twisted it. When the hero withdrew his weapon, the spearhead remained inside the dragon.

"You vile disgusting creature," wailed the maiden.

"It's all right now," called out the prince, who thought she meant the dragon. "It's dead."

"Murderer!" shrieked the maiden, over and over again.

"Oh, shut up, you miserable bitch," the prince shouted.

The prince called to his friends, who were very brave now that the beast was subdued. "Help me haul out the gold before the harpy's old man sees us, and I have to marry her."

It took seven of his band to lift the dragon's body and the other six to roll the golden apple out from under it. They pushed the apple out of the courtyard and didn't stop until they reached the bottom of a steep hill. There they covered themselves and the apple with branches and leaves and hid, sleeping until the next day when they were awakened by the local people celebrating the maiden's release. As the villagers gossiped, drank, and wondered who the brave and lucky lad might be who had won both Eva's hand and the huge golden apple, Prince Eric and his warriors nudged the apple along the ravine and slunk away. They didn't stop for rest until dawn.

When the merchant and his daughter joined the celebration, the people were disappointed: the hero who had pulled off this remarkable feat was nowhere to be seen.

And yet, Eva's father was determined that his daughter would be saved for the man who had freed her. When he talked over the situation with Hilda, he said, "That boy must not have known that besides the gold he would be awarded an even greater jewel."

His wife thought the boy had shown good sense to take the gold and leave Eva, but she didn't say a word. "Perhaps," said Hilda, "it was not a man but an angel that freed Eva." She didn't believe this herself, but she thought that if Aldrich could be convinced of it he might get over his ridiculous idea of saving Eva for a man who didn't want her. At this rate, Hilda feared, the girl would never marry.

"No," said Aldrich, "Eva can describe the lad, and he looked nothing like an angel. Frumpy and dumpy though he may be, a promise is a promise."

The next day the dragon was cut up for stew, and the cook found the prince's spearhead wedged between the beast's sacrum and lumbar column. When Aldrich heard of it, he said that whoever owned the shaft that fit into this spearhead should have his daughter, and none other. He offered a reward for information leading to the whereabouts of the spear and its owner. This led to a number of wild-goose chases. Adventurers presented shafts to the father in hopes of claiming the maiden and the generous dowry. None of the shafts, however, fit the spearhead. After a while, no one tried.

Meanwhile, Eric and his friends hid by day. Night after night they traveled, rolling the golden apple before them. It took them a year to get home. When they finally got to the border, they discovered that their country had been devastated. They talked to the villagers and heard one tragic story after another about the marauding devils who had taken their food, raped their daughters, and stolen whatever they could carry. The people had been enslaved by the kingdom's ancient enemy, and the king had been kidnapped. The people believed in their hearts that he was alive and that he would return to restore order and prosperity.

Seeing the heartbreak of the people, Eric had a new feeling. Shame. Not because he couldn't save his father and his people—with the gold he had obtained he could buy all the warriors it would take to free the king and the kingdom. He was glad he had the gold, of course, but he was ashamed of some of the things he had done on his quest to get it. He blushed to remember the villages of nearby kingdoms he had plundered and the food he and his men had stolen. True, they hadn't stooped so low as to rape virgins or torture men for sport, but he had to ask himself if they had left some villages as destitute as his homeland. He vowed, once he restored his father to the throne, to make amends.

For her part, Eva, who had become accustomed to confinement in the tower, relished her new freedom. She rode her horse around the countryside, expecting a warm welcome from the boys she used to ride with. She found, however, they were no longer boys, but men. If their paths crossed in a field, the men nodded affably and rode on. Her old companions had settled down with wives, land grants, farms and children. When she came across old flames at the market, she found they had little to say to each other. She began to feel that these men had shown their true colors by being too afraid of their mothers to ask for her hand and too cowardly to attempt to free her from the tower.

With little to do, Eva found time heavy on her hands. One of the few people her age in the household was a servant girl. Eva watched from a chair or her bed while Tecla cleaned: scrubbing floors, gathering linen to launder in the river, scuttling to the kitchen to pare vegetables, or running to the barn to milk.

Despite her hard life, Tecla smiled easily, and Eva marveled at her patience. When no one was around to report her to her parents, Eva pitched in to help Tecla with the chores. Once the girl got over the feeling that this was some sort of criticism, the two began to chat.

Eva wondered how Tecla could be so cheerful when her life appeared to be wretched. "Why must you work so hard?"

"We are a large family," said Tecla. "I have three brothers and six sisters, plus a brother who died from hunger. The boys are too young to be much help in the fields, and our allotment is too small for all the mouths it must feed. Most of what's earned by my father's labor goes to our overlord. My mother works harder than I do, taking care of all of us and making beer and cakes to sell. Of course the lord takes his share of those as well. I must help, and I want to."

"Yet you are happy; happier than I," said Eva, "what is your secret?"

"I'm grateful that I have kind mistresses. You and your mother are very good to me. I'm grateful for my kind parents. My father never beats any of us, and my mother has often gone hungry so we would have food."

One day Eva offered Tecla some jewelry. Tecla looked frightened. "I dare not take that, Miss."

"Of course you shall," said Eva.

"And be hung for a thief? If I'm seen with something so grand, someone would snitch to the sheriff. Nine-year-olds are hung for stealing bread."

Eva felt foolish; she hadn't thought of that. Being hung for stealing was not something she had to think about. "I'm sorry," she said. "I'll find another way."

She sought out her father, who was with her mother watching the evening clouds roll over the nearby hills. She asked him to sell some of her gold necklaces. "Whatever for?" asked Aldrich. "I want to help Tecla's family. They're very poor and have many mouths to feed."

"God has ordained rich and poor, that the work of the world be accomplished. If all were rich, who would work?" said Aldrich.

"Couldn't we share out the work and the riches?"

Her father said nothing. His mouth had a grim set. Her mother was quiet as well, but later took Eva aside and asked how many villagers might need help. Hilda said nothing to Aldrich, but prepared food and gathered used clothing from her well-off friends. Eva made the deliveries, and now there were no grass stains on her dress when she returned.

Five years went by. The maiden, although older, was still handsome. Whenever they had a guest, the story of the dragon and the miraculous apple was trotted out. Eva was so tired of the tale that she hardly listened. But one night an abbot on pilgrimage stopped at the hall for the night and claimed that he had already heard it. He said he recognized the story as the same one told in a distant king's hall, give or take a few details. For example, he had heard that the prince was a handsome hero who had saved

his kingdom, but the maiden's beauty and accomplishment were not mentioned at all.

Ha! thought Eva. *Handsome, my foot. That boy looked as sexy as Humpty Dumpty.*

Aldrich was all ears. Trying not to get his hopes up, he asked if the abbot had any idea where the lad lives.

"I know where he comes from, and I know who he is."

So, hurray, thought Eva. *He knows who the jerk is.*

The abbot departed at daybreak the next morning. Aldrich sought out Eva to tell her that as soon as the servants packed their bags and prepared a carriage, they would travel as far as necessary to meet the young man. "For heaven's sake, Daddy," said his daughter, "he must be married by now."

"We don't know that," said Aldrich.

"You should have asked the abbot before dragging me on this fool's errand."

"If he is married, he can release us from our promise, and I will find someone else for you."

"This is humiliating," said Eva.

The very next morning, the father, spearhead in hand and maiden in tow, headed for the far-off kingdom. Eva, despite a certain set to her jaw, didn't argue with her father. She had learned to humor him. At least a trip was a change.

By now Prince Eric's father had been back on his throne for four years. His kingdom thrived. Prince Eric had returned home after wandering the countryside near and far to apologize to all who had been wronged by him and his warriors. Most of these poor souls were so accustomed to being preyed upon by wandering marauders that they had no idea which ones he had led, or even if he had attacked their village. But they didn't let that stop them from accepting his gold.

They talked about their lives over the years. After a while they got around to that *fateful* night

Every night since he had been rescued, the old king remembered his unknown benefactors in his prayers. He believed Eva's family were, in large part, responsible for his deliverance from the hands of his enemy. When he heard the family were coming, he instructed his court to show them every courtesy. As Eva and her father walked through the gates, the people lined the streets and cheered. The king himself came out to welcome them.

The prince, old enough now to be charming even to a woman he wasn't particularly fond of, greeted the maiden and her father graciously. Eva noticed that even though he was older he looked a lot better now that he wasn't wearing an overstuffed, pitch-covered leather fleece.

At the feast that night, Eva sat next to Prince Eric and across from his sister. Eric inquired solicitously about her trip. Eva didn't particularly want to talk to the prince, but she did want to find out if he was married. She hoped the answer would put an end to this nonsense. She waited for the right moment. Eva first asked about the kingdom's harvest and the security of their border, then she moved on to lighter topics.

"Have pancake races caught on here?" The prince and his sister had never heard of them. "Do you dance after dinner?" They usually listened to poetry or a story.

Finally, she asked, "Will I have the pleasure of meeting your wife, sir?"

Prince Eric's face clouded, and Eva noticed his expressive hazel eyes. "I lost my wife two years ago. The baby as well." Eva was genuinely sorry, for more than one reason. To change the subject, the prince's sister asked Eva if she enjoyed attending court at home, but that was awkward as well. "Merchants' daughters are not invited," said Eva.

They muddled through the rest of dinner, if not connecting,

at least avoiding further embarrassment. Afterward, a lyre played in the background while the evening's raconteur told the story of the dragon yet again. Eva caught the prince's eye. "You should have seen yourself," she said, "trying to keep your footing on the dragon's back."

"It wasn't easy, I can tell you," said the prince.

"You were as white as death," said the maiden, "and you kept shouting to your men that you had everything under control."

"Just trying to convince myself," said the prince.

"I can still see you thrashing about. You looked like a dumpy old woman beating a rug. What were you wearing, anyway?"

The prince laughed. "Never mind," he said.

"As a hero, I'm afraid you weren't quite what I had pictured," said Eva.

"And I'm afraid what I did that night was somewhat more heroic than what I'd done en route," the prince said.

"But to be fair, I guess I looked somewhat ludicrous myself."

"Not a bit," he said. "You looked quite fetching standing at the window with your hair sticking out in all directions shrieking like a screech owl."

The maiden laughed. "Hard to believe I was so ridiculous. But believe it or not, I felt sorry for the dragon."

They shook their heads. "We were so young," they both said, still smiling.

The prince looked at Eva. He liked the shape of her mouth. "You were sweet," he said, "to care so much about a reptile."

Eva looked at the prince. His cheekbones were cut at just the right angle. "You were the only man brave enough to rescue me."

They gazed into each other's eyes. Her father noticed.

"Stop everything," said Aldrich.

"Now what?" said Eva.

A Perfect Fit

"We have to check his spear."

The prince called a servant to fetch his spear. Prince Eric removed its head. The one Eva's father handed him was a perfect fit. Eva was relieved that her father had the tact not to mention his inane marriage proposition in front of the entire court.

Aldrich said nothing to her about it when they were alone, and she began to think that he must have finally figured out it was futile.

At the same time, the king was so cordial and had thought of so many outings and entertainments that Eva had to agree it would have seemed rude to leave too quickly. One day the king planned to take his visitors to see a distant estate. Eva preferred riding to bumping along in a carriage and, as they were about to leave, she asked a groom if she might have a horse. If the king or prince was surprised by this request, they hid it well. Riding like the wind across the countryside, Eva felt more like herself than she had for a very long time. The next time they went on an excursion, Eric rode alongside her.

Conversation during dinner had become comfortable, even congenial. Eva looked forward to the after-dinner stories, and as they were told, she and Eric often exchanged glances.

One night they heard about sea monsters that devoured ships and crews until a fearless warrior swam across the sea underwater to kill him. Eva didn't believe the part about the way he killed the monster. The tale had it that the warrior's sword had rusted, so he had to dispatch the creature by biting it on the neck. Eric wondered how the man had held his breath long enough to cross the sea. Nevertheless, they thought it was an entertaining tale. "After all," said Eric, "most people don't believe in dragons anymore, and we know they exist."

"Or used to," said Eva. "Maybe you wiped out the last one."

"I suppose it had to happen," said Eric. They both thought there was something a little sad about that. "How can a young man today test his valor?" asked Eric. "Or prove his devotion to his lady?"

"You weren't exactly devoted to me," said Eva. They both laughed, but there was something in Eric's eye that made Eva blush and look away.

On another night they heard a romantic tale about a prince, cursed by one of those evil fairies that were once so prevalent. He was saved by the baker's daughter. "I like this one," said Eva. "It's nice to hear a story that doesn't feature a pathetic, helpless girl."

"So, in your story," asked Eric, "it would be a traveling girl who kisses the knight and breaks his trance?"

"Sure, why not?

The days turned into weeks. At dinner one night, the prince complimented Eva on her horsemanship. She reached for a way to return his praise. "My lord," she said, "I've noticed you cut a fine figure jousting with the lads."

"We are practicing for the fighting season. Come watch us tomorrow, and afterward we can go riding."

The next day, Eva noticed that many of the young ladies came to watch the men practice. The ladies giggled and tittered and picked their favorites. The men showed off. When Eric defeated an opponent not far from where Eva sat, she was flattered to see the prince smile and wink at her before he took his bow.

After the match, Eva waited while Eric and his men went over the afternoon's skirmishes. By the time they finished, the sun was low in the sky. Eva was beginning to think that Eric had forgotten all about his invitation, when she saw a groom arrive with two horses. Eric took their reins and walked over to Eva. "How about a race?" he asked.

Eva laughed, jumped on one of the horses, and galloped off. She was halfway across the field before Eric was in the saddle. But still, when it came to riding, he was no slouch. He caught up with her when she had to slow down to enter the woodland on the other side of the field. He managed to pull ahead by one length as the road narrowed.

The road was good for a while, and they kept up a canter. Twilight deepened and the wood became denser. The moon had not yet risen, and the forest was dark. Bushes encroached. The road, now little more than a path, was criss-crossed with roots. Branches from trees drooped lower and closer to their heads, until, finally, one of them must have hit Eric right across the forehead.

He fell off his horse. Eva, close behind, reined in her horse and dismounted.

"What happened?"

Eric said nothing. Eva knelt beside him to investigate. Eric moaned. "My head—"

"Where does it hurt?" asked Eva.

He put his hand on the far side of his head. She reached across him to examine the bump.

"I don't feel anything," she said. "I'll go back to the palace and get help."

"No!" said Eric. He grasped her hand. "I'll be all right soon. Stay with me. The branch hit my chest, too." He moved her hand to his torso. "I think I broke a rib. What do you think?"

She felt his chest. It felt fine to Eva. Very fine. "That's helping," said Eric, putting a hand on her hip. "I'm beginning to feel a little better."

"Where is that branch that hit you?" asked Eva.

"It must be around," said Eric.

"I don't see it."

"It's kind of dark," said Eric.

"Not anymore. The moon has risen."

"Oh. Maybe it was an arrow," he said.

"What?!"

"From Cupid's bow," said the prince.

Eva laughed, but then her gaze fastened onto Eric's. He was looking at her exactly the way she wanted a man to look at her. Eric pulled her toward him, and she kissed him. It was a long while before they returned to the castle.

The foreign merchant who had sold the small gold apple and the baby dragon to Aldrich had been right. In the end, those gifts did bring Eva good fortune. The maiden and the prince were married, and as old as they were, they were blessed with six healthy sons and two daughters. And they lived happily ever after. Even if, like most couples, they confused each other most of the time.

Books by Elaine Drew

Courting Trouble
Nun Too Clever
A Knight's Bad Day
Damsel's Dilemma

elainedrew.com